WALT DISNEY PRODUCTIONS
presents

ROBIN HOOD WINS AGAIN

Random House New York

First American Edition. Copyright © 1983 by Walt Disney Productions. All rights reserved under International and Pan-American Copyright Conventions. Published in the United States by Random House, Inc., New York, and simultaneously in Canada by Random House of Canada Limited, Toronto. Originally published in Denmark as ROBIN HOOD OG LADY MARIAN by Gutenberghus Gruppen, Copenhagen. ISBN: 0-394-85830-1 Manufactured in the United States of America   3 4 5 6 7 8 9 0   A B C D E F G H I J K

Book Club Edition

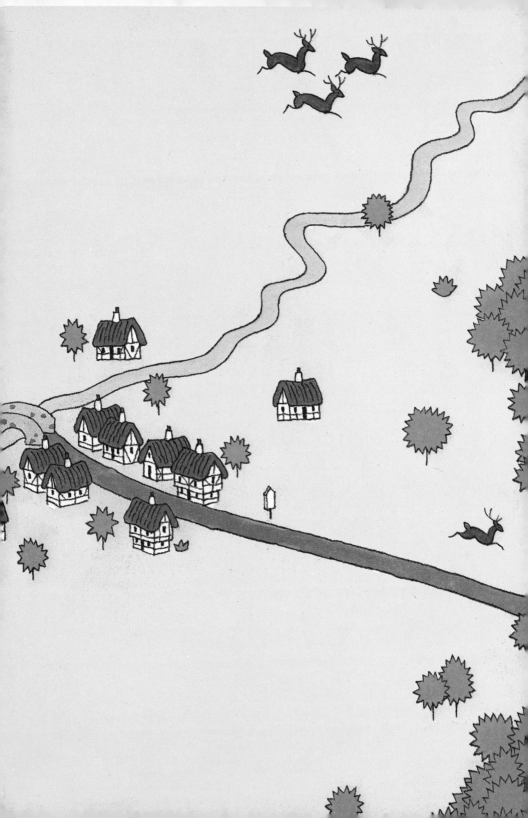

Deep in Sherwood Forest lived Robin Hood.
He hid there from Prince John.
Robin Hood took money from the rich
and gave it to the poor.
So Prince John called him an outlaw.
But the poor called him a hero.

Friar Tuck and Little John lived
with Robin Hood in the forest.
Skippy Rabbit often came to visit.

Robin Hood had another friend.
Her name was Maid Marian.
She lived in Prince John's castle
with Lady Kluck.
Prince John did not want Maid Marian
to see Robin Hood.

One day Maid Marian was feeling
very sad.

"Oh, Klucky," she said. "It's been so
long since I've seen Robin Hood. I think
he has forgotten me."

"Don't be sad," said Lady Kluck.
"Robin Hood would never forget you."

Lady Kluck was quite right.

For at that very moment Robin Hood was writing a letter to Maid Marian.

Robin wanted to meet her at the fair in Nottingham.

Robin Hood called to his friend Skippy.
"Please take this letter to Maid Marian,"
he said. "Don't let anyone in the castle
see it."

"You can trust me,"
said Skippy. "I will
be careful."

Skippy ran as fast as he could through the forest.

When he got close to the castle, he hid the letter in his hat.

At the castle the gate was open.
A wagon was going inside.
Skippy followed it into the castle.
He pretended that he had nothing to hide.

Skippy sneaked into the big courtyard.
He saw the guard on the wall.
"Good, he's asleep," said Skippy.

There was no one else in the courtyard.
Skippy tiptoed quietly over to
Maid Marian's window.
There was a strong vine that led
straight up to it.

Skippy made sure that nobody was looking.

He quickly climbed up the vine.

He called Maid Marian, but no one answered.

The ladies had stepped away.

So Skippy left Robin's letter on the windowsill.

Then he climbed down the vine.

The guard was not really asleep.
He had kept one eye open.
He saw everything that Skippy did!
He went to get the letter from
the windowsill.

"Hmmm," he said. "I'll bet Robin Hood
is sending a letter to Maid Marian.
I'll just take this to Prince John."

The guard rushed to Prince John's room.
Two big guards blocked the way.
"Let me in," said the courtyard guard.
"I have a letter to show Prince John."
And he rushed past them.

Prince John was counting tax money.

His advisor, Sir Hiss, and the sheriff were watching.

"What is-s this-s?" asked Sir Hiss when the courtyard guard burst in.

"I have a letter from Robin Hood to Maid Marian," said the guard.

"Let me have the letter," said the sheriff.
He read it aloud to Prince John.

Dear Marian,

    I have not forgotten you.
I want to see you soon.

    Please ask Prince John
to take you to the fair in
Nottingham today.

    I will meet you in the
green tent.

       Love,

       Robin Hood

"Aha!" said the sheriff. "This is our
chance to catch Robin Hood. Bring Maid
Marian to the tent and I will grab him
there."

"Good idea," said Prince John.

"Be careful, sire,"
said Sir Hiss.
"Robin Hood has
tricked us-s before."

"Quiet!" said
Prince John.

Maid Marian did not know about the letter.
And so she did not know what Prince John
and the sheriff were planning.

"Do you think Robin Hood will ever come
for me, Klucky?" she asked sadly.

She looked at a picture of Robin Hood that
hung in her closet.

"I'm sure that Robin will come,"
said Lady Kluck.

Just then there was
a knock at the door.
    "Someone is coming,"
said Lady Kluck. "Quickly,
close the closet!"

Lady Kluck opened the bedroom door.
There stood Prince John and Sir Hiss.
"Ah, Lady Kluck and Maid Marian,"
said Prince John. "I am going to the fair
in Nottingham town. Do you want to go
with me?"

"Do you, Marian?" asked Lady Kluck.
"Oh, yes! I'm tired of staying in
the castle all day," said Maid Marian.

"Good!" said Prince John.
"Meet me downstairs in
ten minutes."
And he and Sir Hiss
hurried out.

But Lady Kluck did not trust
Prince John or Sir Hiss.
So she listened at the door.
She heard them talking in the hall.

"This-s is the best trap we have ever set for Robin Hood," said Sir Hiss.

"We will catch him this time," said Prince John.

Prince John and Sir Hiss did a merry little dance.

Now Lady Kluck was worried. How could she warn Robin Hood?

Lady Kluck rushed to the window.
She saw Skippy Rabbit down in
the courtyard.

She hurried downstairs to talk to Skippy.
"Go tell Robin Hood that the sheriff
is planning to catch him at the fair,"
said Lady Kluck.

Skippy was off in a flash.

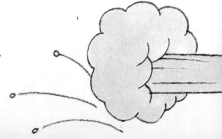

Skippy ran as fast as he
could through the forest.

He was all tired out when
he got to Robin's camp.
"What's up?" asked Robin Hood.

"Prince John and the sheriff are going
to catch you at the fair," said Skippy.
Robin Hood laughed and said,
"We will see who
gets caught . . ."

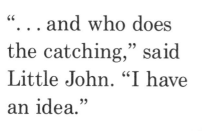

". . . and who does
the catching," said
Little John. "I have
an idea."

At the castle the sheriff was ready
to leave for the fair.

"I will wait at the green tent with
my men," said the sheriff to Prince John.
"Robin Hood won't get away this time."

"I can't wait to catch him!" Prince John
said. "At last Maid Marian will see that
Robin Hood is not so smart."

Prince John stroked
his beard and smiled.

Maid Marian and Lady
Kluck came down into
the courtyard.

"You may ride in
my private coach," said
Prince John.

His coach was pulled
by elephants.

As usual, Prince John was traveling
with his bags of gold.

That worried Sir Hiss.

What if outlaws stopped the coach?

Lady Kluck was worried too—but for
a different reason.

Robin Hood was in danger!

But Lady Kluck did not need to worry.
Robin Hood and Little John had planned
a good trick.
They tied a huge net in the trees.

They waited until Prince John's coach
was right under the net.

Then they
quickly cut
the net loose.

The net crashed down.
It fell over the coach and the elephants.
Now Prince John and Sir Hiss were caught!

The elephants were caught too.
They could not pull the coach.

Prince John looked out.
"What is going on?"
he roared.

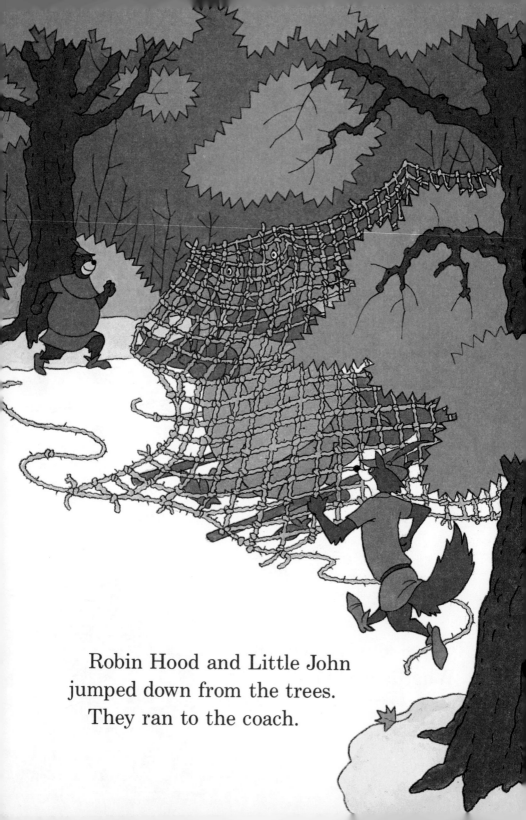

Robin Hood and Little John
jumped down from the trees.
They ran to the coach.

Little John lifted the net.

Robin Hood opened the coach curtains.

"Good day, Prince John," said Robin.

"Welcome to Sherwood Forest."

Prince John was too surprised to answer.

First Robin Hood helped
Lady Kluck out of the coach.
Then he helped Maid Marian.

And Little John helped Prince John's gold
out of the coach.
Then they all ran off to Robin's camp
in the forest.

That night there was a big party in
Robin's camp.

Robin Hood danced with Maid Marian.
And everybody sang and clapped.

"Tomorrow that gold goes to the poor,"
said Robin.

Late that night the sheriff got back to the castle.

"We waited all day at the fair," he said to Prince John. "But Robin Hood never turned up."

"He turned up all right—in Sherwood Forest," said Prince John. "He took all my gold. How come Robin Hood always wins?"

And Prince John sighed.